Morning
Arrow_____

Morning
Arrow———————

Nanabah Chee Dodge

illustrated by Jeffrey Lungé—————

F
Do

Lothrop, Lee & Shepard Co. / New York

1   2   3   4   5   79   78   77   76   75

Library of Congress Cataloging in Publication Data

Dodge, Nanabah Chee.
    Morning Arrow.

    SUMMARY: Chronicles the life of a ten-year-old Navajo boy and his
blind grandmother living in the Monument Valley of Utah.
    [1. Navaho Indians—Fiction. 2. Indians of North America—Fiction] I.
Lungé, Jeffrey, illus. II. Title.
PZ7.D67Mo   [E]   74-20977
ISBN 0-688-41687-X
ISBN 0-688-51687-4 lib. bdg.

To my parents
with love from their daughter

*A*way in the north part of Arizona and New Mexico is the homeland of America's largest tribe —the Navaho. Clear up into the foothills of Colorado and Utah, neatly nesting beneath the wet skies are the Utes and their neighbors, the Apaches—and the Navaho (Diné). My home is in the Monument Valley of Utah.

Each day I wake up to the singing of Sídeā, the bird of dawn; unlike others, Sídea has golden wings that become darker in the sunlight.

Sometimes I can hear his feathers softly shoring in space—like the eagle, he beats his way rudely.

When you are ten and the country turns velvet green, the beauty of spring matches your age.

I run, arms apart—legs going one way—breathing the good air in and out—never knowing what air is!

I feel as if there is no other world near or far like this. I know of no toy-thing but still I dream and find magic, playing with the shadows or being a bird with endless forms or maybe a leafless tree.

I know I can be all these things. Morning Arrow is my name. I live with my grandmother. I stay with her because I like her—she makes me very happy. Today I go after water with two buckets—there is a waterhole down the hill where the tree is bent backward.

I feel the sand surfacing the ground—sometimes it just plays rather modestly—at times I gather it in my palm and throw it into mid-air—watch it bounce back in front of my face and laugh out loud.

The bees fuss about me. I hope they understand that I have come to get water. My body tells me to run, but fear stops me!

"Go away! Go away!" I stop shouting and they leave.

After I got the water my grandmother asked if we could walk about.

"Yes," I said.

She is half blind so I lead her with a stick that is not too long, or short.

She pointed to the Monument Valley and asked if the butte was there.

"Yes."

"Do you see any yucca fruit?"

"No," I said.

We walked slowly around our empty yard which cradled virgin grounds.

We live in a mud house we call our home— Hooghan, house everlasting—with the doorway to the East where the sun always rises. The iron stove stands in the center of the one room on the earth floor.

We have comfortable beds made out of sheepskin and goatskin.

Grandmother cooks well. I like her green corn bread which takes a day to make. She sends me out to gather herbs.

At supper Grandmother laid out her tablecloth —once a flour sack—and odd dishes which she dearly loves. They came from cereal boxes. We had lamb jerky and wild tea.

11

At night the sky glued its face upon the earth, making all things alike, while the heavens danced with thousands of lights.

"Where is the Big Dipper?" Grandmother asked.

"Over behind the mountain, not like days ago." She shook her head. I know she understood.

"Full moon or half?"

"There is no moon, just stars," I said.

"Where is the Bear Man this time?"

"Over your head—how do you know that there is a Bear Man up there?" I asked.

"I grew up under this universe. I've studied the stars and know the names of each one and where they are," she said, as she pointed with the stick.

Soon the days will turn warm and the sunrises will please my eyes—such beauty I can't miss. And there will be sunsets to paint the buttes dusty red. Each bush will cast a giant shadow and all the shadows will march into the valley.

I watched the earth grow into purple-gray clothing before it silenced off into darkness.

Summertime on the reservation is a fun time for all Navaho boys and girls. Those who were

off at school now return. It is also the season for Piñon nuts off the Piñon tree. We go miles with blankets and buckets and old potato sacks to put the nuts in. Eight miles from Grandmother's home are lots of Piñon trees—they stand old and aged. They begin at the foot of the canyon and go far into the canyon.

I walk *"Shimá sáni"* (Grandmother). I go ahead and lead her to the place where the road divides. There we wait for "Mister Two Face," a medicine man. People call him "Two Face" because he sees the good and the troubled of each person. He drives a wagon with a yellow horse and a donkey pulling in front.

We shake the Piñon tree and pick the nuts that have fallen. Everyone takes part. Grandmother put the nuts in a pan and let them roast over the small flame. One can smell Piñons far away— listen to the popping sound.

One day my father came over. He had gathered a small herd of sheep and goats for us. Though Grandmother couldn't see them she could feel each tail, each ear.

The lambs grew to sheep size. We clipped off their tails and sheared their coats so the wool could be spun, dyed, washed, and woven into rugs and yarn. All day long I'd watch her pull the yarn through each part of the loom, as the colors graded into a design.

"Morning Arrow, how am I doing?"

"All right," I said.

She kept fingering the edge, feeling her way. How I love her.

One day I went off to find dye for her. "Now remember the purple sage and buds off the yellow wild flower to make the color—also dig up the yucca roots."

I sang, "Purple sage! Yellow flower! Yucca roots!" on and on. How I enjoy running with my thoughts—away—away—away.

I jumped on the Eagle Rock. Here the eagle sits in daylight enjoying his dream, while his eyes tour behind each rock, bush, for anything that moves. I watched him feed his hunger. To me he is all brave.

After the Eagle Rock I came on a tree with a bee-hive. For fun I shook the tree hard until the

hive fell to the ground. I was teasing the bees. I grabbed the hive and ran, leaping like a deer, knowing the bees were after me.

Breaking off a piece of the hive I put it up another tree. As the bees circled about, I raced toward the waterhole. I made a clay box, let it dry, and placed the rest of the hive inside where it would be safe, I hoped.

I found the purple sage and the yellow flower and the yucca root. Now the eagle combed my head—around and around he sailed—as his wings shadowed the sagebrush. I so wanted to hide. I pulled my coat over my head.

"I have done wrong!" I said to myself. "Why should the eagle be angry at me?" Grandmother says, "Don't ever let the eagle frighten you—or the owl—or the hawk. Talk to them, they understand." Suddenly I felt my heart pound hard. I fell to the ground where my tears dried quickly on the rock.

When the sun sets in the Monument Valley, the buttes become stone castles to human eyes. Grandmother walks with her stick poking at space and both ears aware of things unseen.

"Morning Arrow, you shouldn't feel ashamed. Come, tell me what you've dreamed up today? I sent you away happy and now you come home sad-eyed?" She smiled tenderly and lovingly.

"I found the purple sage, the yellow flower, and the yucca roots and piled them into a sack. But then I was frightened by the eagle."

"Why did it take you so long to come home?"

"Well—" I said.

"Something tells me you are a very proud man. What else have you done?"

"How can you tell?"

"By your steps, by the way you walk—almost singing."

"Yes," I answered. "I saw the Elephant Foot Butte which I have heard about in our legend. They say in Navaho the one who climbs to the top of Elephant Foot Butte will be rich because the ancient Diné saw a rainbow there. Grandmother, there is supposed to be gold piled as high as your ears there—it is the house of the richest rich! Some day I will climb it."

"Good, now let's go to sleep," Grandmother said.

I watched the flame fight for its life to stillness.

All summer long Grandmother sat beside her loom, using her fingers as if they had hidden eyes. I herded our sheep up and down the sandy path, always looking out for coyotes and wild dogs. Mósí (the cat) spent most of her day with the herd. I played with my marbles by allowing them to go free, or by rubbing them against each other. This kept me busy.

In the afternoons I returned, seeing that each sheep and goat was in before I went to Grandmother. The time came when she finished her rug. It was beautiful—it was all the colors of the rainbow.

"We will sell the rug at the trading post tomorrow. We must see more friends and go more places."

"Yes," I said. "The white man, is he a good man?"

She laughed a little. "Tomorrow you will see your first white friend."

"Have you seen one, Grandmother?"

"I've lived with them and they are only strange

23

because we look strange to their eyes. One day you, Morning Arrow, will walk among them—a proud man you will be—for the door is always open to knowledge." She pulled her shawl gently over her head. She was a figure of such magnificent humility. I followed.

The trading post was twenty-five miles away in the Chuska Mountains of Arizona. We went on foot to the divided road. Both forks of the road were wagon paths.

"There are two twisted trees next to the road. I see them," I told Grandmother.

"That road we take," she said. She carried a sack of bread which she had baked for our lunch. The shawl over her back was tattooed with too many holes. Her only skirt swept the ground. Sometimes she would stop and pull it up—one side hung lower—it was French silk and had been a gift to her. Her blouse was green velvet. It was still beautiful. Before her eyes darkened she had admired the jeweled colors of clothing. She stopped and re-tied her saddle shoes and said, "Find me pretty shoestrings at the trading post."

"Yes," I nodded.

As I carried the rug it became heavier and heavier! The sun passed over the Chuska Mountain and everywhere sagebrush scent filled the air. There was a gentle somberness I could feel. It was somewhat frightening. One long road remained between us and the trading post.

"Is that it?" I yelled.

"Dó you see a cottonwood tree?" she asked.

"Yes."

"We are there then." She led me, this time.

The stone house stood tough-like, almost rude, in a country like this. Wagons and horses were parked beneath the cottonwood. My stomach was eager to go to war against good bologna and white bread. The door shut behind us. My eyes danced from left to right, right to left!

There were things I had never seen or touched. Many items were tied to the stone house wall. Hats, blankets, pans, buckets, cereal boxes, flour sacks, lard cans, coffee, shoes, pots, ropes, new saddles, clothes for everyone, boots, full sugar bags, and jewelry, all Navaho. Everything was expensive.

"Yá'teh simá háádéé?" the trader asked.

("Hello, Grandmother, where are you from?")

"Nilei tazhito'ji áíy díídó shiy áázd," she said. ("Way over from Elephant Foot area. Me and Sonny Boy live there.")

I watched the white man's face as he smiled at me. He rubbed my head. He had marble blue eyes like the sky and his skin had a red cast with light bouncing off it.

"Grandmother is blind," I said.

"She made this?"

"Yes."

The trader unfolded the rug and looked at it closely. The rest he told with his eyes.

"Nizhó nígo." ("Very beautiful.") *"Díkwíí?"* ("How much?")

"Neezná din b'éesobaah ilii doolee," she said. ("It is worth one hundred dollars.")

"Oh, that's too much."

He thought a bit, as I kept my eyes on his face.

"Ná' nisin—tso stsídiin 'ashdla?" ("How about seventy-five dollars?")

Grandmother looked for me. She fanned her hand seven times, counting in her way. "I can't see, but we must live. We need groceries (ch-

26

...

'iyáán bááh)—bread, meat, canned fruits, a sack of flour—" She pulled her shawl over her neck and said, *"Ouu'nē' nisin tso stsídiin 'ashdla."* ("Seventy-five dollars it is.")

She looked toward me again and brushed off my dusty old hat. With part of the seventy-five dollars she bought me a new hat, cowboy boots and a shirt with pants.

Then suddenly I thought about her. She must have something too!

"How much is that shawl?" I pointed to one hanging on the wall.

"That is a Pendleton. It's very expensive," the trader said.

I straightened up and said, "I am rich!"

"All right, Sonny, it's thirty-five dollars."

I stopped and moved away from him. I saw other Navaho standing around. They seemed strange. I looked at the shawl and my heart began to cry out loud. I must be a man and not get frightened by unfamiliar faces.

"I'll be back," I said in a low voice.

"Okay." The white man nodded, his face all smiles. He gave us our sacks of groceries. *"Ahé heé*

—*ággee'n.*" ("Thank you and so long," he said.)

We ate lunch on the banks of the cottonwood forest. I had a soda pop—such a strange color but so, so good a taste. Afterward we started home. We camped near the so-called Talking Hill.

"Grandmother, are all white people like that man?"

"No, just some."

"Grandmother, did you see. . . ? I saw a man buy a saddle and fabric for his family. Does that mean he is rich? Maybe he found the gold in Elephant Foot, Grandmother?" I thought while I watched the stars glide across the heavens. Perhaps I should not dream so much.

Days later my father came and asked if we wanted to go to the Tribal Fair.

"Yes," we said.

I dressed up in my new Navaho costume for this was my first fair. Grandmother wore a velvet costume and her deerskin moccasins. She also wore her silver and turquoise jewelry. We left two days before the fair started in my father's wagon pulled by two black horses. By the third day we got there. There were wagons and wagons of people from all over. Navaho sold rugs and turquoise jewelry from their tents. Others came with squashes and melons and cooked ears of corn. Grandmother met all her old friends. I entered the watermelon race and won two melons. I won in the tug-of-war, all for twenty-five cents! And then I raced until I was breathless. This time thirty-five cents was given to the winner and also a case of soda pop! In the day we saw the rodeo and in the evening the "Squaw Dance," with the men singing until dawn. It was the music that I remember the most.

It was my first fair and what fun! I did nothing but sleep on the way back home.

Soon the days turned cooler and cooler. We gathered and stored the firewood and herbs— wild tea, onions, sagebrush and gum sap from pine, not to overlook cedar chips for a strong fire. Winter was on the way.

One day I got up early and without Grandmother's knowledge I started out to the trading

post to see about that shawl. My ram moved slowly. My stomach cried when I was near the trading post.

"Well, *yát'éh.*" ("Hello.") The white man asked where my grandmother was. But I only listened to what I wanted to hear.

"I want to put this on that . . . Penlytin . . . sir," I said, with a stiff upper lip and handed him the money I had saved.

"Yes. Let's count. Twenty-five plus—(I watched him finger the silver)—thirty-five makes sixty cents—a long way from thirty-five dollars! You like that shawl, don't you?"

"Yes."

"Well, I need more than this."

"What do you mean, sir?"

"I need the price of three live lambs (*dibé*). Look, what is your name?"

"Morning Arrow," I said.

"You should be in school. Wait! Did you come on foot like you and your grandmother did before?"

"No." I pouted and left with his voice echoing in my ears.

My eyes shut out the light while I stood facing the stone house, crying away my hunger and disappointment. I will never be rich, even if I climb the Elephant Foot. No one believes!

"Whose ram is that?" shouted the trader.

"Mine."

He looked at me and then at the ram. "You rode him? Who named you?"

I eyed his Western boots and bowed meekly. "Grandmother."

"You are brave, Sonny—just you and your grandmother living out there. She is blind and you are her eyes. The more I live out here among your people the more I am becoming a Diné. Well, it's getting late." He went back in.

I thought about what he had said and all at once I had a brave idea—the ram! I rushed into the stone house, smiling my way.

"Huh, what now?" asked the trader.

"How much would you pay for the ram?"

"Oh, he's nice and fat—good wool—young too." He studied my face, which beamed a bit. He leaned over his glass case. "You make a good chief trader," he said, and he took down the shawl. "Okay, the shawl for the ram. Pen—ly—tin. Say it fast—Pendleton! Pendleton!"

I rubbed my hands over the beautiful turquoise Pendleton and smelled its freshness.

"How are you going to get home?" he asked.

"Walk," I said.

I walked with my shoulders held high—my nose to the sky. It was a sudden dream. I could imagine Grandmother tucking at the shawl. She would wrap it around both of us and how we would love it—as if it were clothing. She would know it by its fresh smell. She might even get to see it in one of her nightly dreams. I was a bit out of breath for the wind kept offsetting my walking. The air was filled with coldness. *"Eíyee',"* I said.

I huddled to a tree while the dark shadows of winter covered the earth. I embraced the shawl so nothing would happen to it. I knew I did this without Grandmother's knowledge and imagined eyes that watched me from all sides. Fear danced in my mind and ears. "Why did I—why did I sell the ram? No—I gave the ram for the shawl. He is the father to my father's herd. Now the ram will be without children, he will feel sad—very sad.

Why did the trader have to see him? Why do I do these things? I felt big with words. But Grandmother needs a new shawl—hers are so old—why did I come?"

I must go back and get the ram. I will keep the shawl too. I wept as the wind was upon me. The trees grew to a monster size as I edged my way back to the trading post, but I wasn't certain of my way. My eyes flashed only on the road while my foot hit the road, small but brave—feeling my way like Grandmother does in daylight.

The snow fell in small patches. Once in awhile it would send off a tiny light that naked eyes could magnify. The wind blew even more. It sang at my misery. Somehow it played louder in a numb ear. There was warmth coming from within my body—at times I would blow that warmth into my hands. I was too cold and very tired and my stomach replied—hunger pain! I remember falling down, holding the shawl next to my heart.

"Morning Arrow? Morning Arrow?"
I opened my eyes. "Where am I?" I said.
"Hello, Sonny. . ."

"Where am I?"

"You are here," said the white man, whose face I had not forgotten.

I looked at the ceiling. *"Da hooghan?"* ("Is this your home?")

"Ao' bilaga'ana hooghan," he said. ("Yes, this is my home.") He smiled and yawned a lot.

I missed the shawl. "Where is the Pendleton?"

"The shawl is at your feet—and your ram ran off—I think he is home, wherever that is." He touched my head with his white palm.

"Did you find me or did I find you?"

"Well, I found you sleeping beside a beautiful white horse."

I looked into his eyes. "I have no white horse."

"Well, then, you should get one," he joked.

White horse. I turned to keep warm and my eyes pushed me into sleep. White horse!

The next day I left quietly. The snow was matted down like a carpet. The door closed gently as I carried out the shawl. I tucked it under my arm. For awhile I thought that the shawl really belonged to me and my grandmother. Such expense called for right thinking. As the sun beamed over

the Chuska Mountain I began to see things as real
—for to a Navaho reality is to be honest with
oneself. One's judgment over a box of candy
might be the lifeline between hunger and starva-
tion. Everything is a magnificent duel in which it
is all right to honor material thought but to be
overrun by a wishful passion is not my teaching.
I could hear my grandmother say, "Morning Arrow, you dream too much. Don't fill your driven
pride."

I caressed the shawl again. Its turquoise color
ran together with shades of orange and rust. It
had white fringes. Tears begged inside me—
please, hurry and take me home. I walked into the
trading post and placed the Pendleton back on
the wall. I stood and looked as it hugged the wall.
Then I remembered that Grandmother wanted
new shoestrings. I found a pair and left my money
on the counter.

I ran out, marking a new trail. I was thankful
for the comfort of the trader's home. It was a great
honor to have stayed there.

I heard a noise behind me. It was my ram cut-
ting through the snow. Was I happy to see him.

41

We went back into our valley. How the snow had dressed every bare branch and stick. Smoke came up from our *hooghan* and curled into space. I could smell the stew and bubbling fry bread. Grandmother was kneeling down and pouring her tea and mine.

"*Yá't'eh shimá sáni.*" ("Hello, Grandmother.")

Her nose pointed down, her eyes away, and she spoke softly. "That ram ran off and you went after him?"

"Yes," I nodded.

"I was worried but I knew you would both be back. It snowed last night."

"Yes."

"You have to watch that ram, he wanders off."

"Yes, Grandmother," I said.

We had our tea. She pulled her skirt over her knees to keep warm.

"Oh," I said, "I have your shoestrings."

"Thank you so much. I need them."

I watched her weave them in and out.

"*Ahé'hee' shiyáázh*, thank you," she said, as she tossed her old shawl over her head. She kept warm that way.

I told her that the shoestrings were orange like

the fruit. She said she liked them. She laid out the dishes for our food. Her fingers touched each, felt each crack on the faces of the plates. I often wondered if her eyes would ever see anything again —for they had life beyond those dark circles. I watched them very closely.

During winter the reservation is all alone with peace. The mountains lock arms with the small hills. The valley wears an unsoiled gown to match her neighbors. When the creek runs in spring one can hear it rush. Now only silence is left. Wherever I look tiny sparkles like broken glass carpet the ground.

The sheep nibble at the branches of a sagebrush and at winter leaves that hang overhead. I put bells around their necks so I can hear them at a distance. Now their coats are five inches thick. Some are old and some younger. Among them are goats with horns and long shaggy coats.

As for Elephant Foot Butte, the snow had placed a white crown over the top, only for the sun to bathe it off. I climbed to the top! I found richness in the climbing.

The jackrabbit painted his way over the hard

winter snow. He was the only artist. The eagle soared into the ash-colored sky. I know he is out to find a new home in a windowless cave. "See you next year!"

It seems so empty, this world about me. I feel that Grandmother and I are the only two left here. I wonder how it is in the white man's world. With that thought in my mind I gathered my herd and went home.

I heard a strange sound, like the gunning of a truck. I saw a truck leaving our *hooghan*. It was the trader. My eyes rushed after him but my legs forgot how to work.

"Grandmother," I yelled, "did the trader come for the ram?"

"*Nooda shiwéé,*" ("No, my child") she said as she tossed the turquoise Pendleton shawl over her head. "He gave this to me. It smells so fresh, it's warm. I feel very rich." Her eyes gave tears.

My heart grew hot. I chased the truck, flapping both arms like wings, jumping over snow-covered bushes. "Hey," I kept on saying, "Hey," until the truck stopped. Breathless I said, "Thank you." (*"Ahehee'"*).

I shook his hand, all the time smiling, and his wife's hand too. Mine was cold.

"Here, these are for you. Merry Christmas, Morning Arrow." He took off his dark glasses that turned everything into dark green.

"*Aay' niz hónígo.* ("Very good, very beautiful.") *T'óó shíí*, mine!"

"Yes, Sonny." He said I looked good in them. I believed him.

We shook hands again. His were warmer than mine.

"Well, Morning Arrow, wait until the bad weather clears before you dream of other things!"

"Yes."

He said goodbye.

I watched him drive off. The truck left a wide trail. I ran back to Grandmother. She stood with her stick and her shawl wrapped around her. It swayed like her jewels. She was happy and very proud.

She said, "Take me for a walk."

I did.

She touched my glasses. "How does the world look to you behind them?"

"Very, very beautiful," I said.

It is the time of the year when all the birds turn and fly away. I wish them a happy journey and a safe return to their beginning here in the spring.